Dotty

BY ERICA S. PERL

ILLUSTRATED BY JULIA DENOS

Abrams Books for Young Readers
New York

This book is dedicated to teachers,
dreamers, and friends true blue
who stick like glue.
—E.S.P.

For my enviable sisters, Christa and Anna,
with the *real* imaginary friends.
—J.D.

The illustrations in this book were made with brush ink
and a bit of Photoshop here and there.

Library of Congress Cataloging-in-Publication Data

Perl, Erica S.
Dotty / by Erica S. Perl ; illustrated by Julia Denos.
p. cm.
Summary: Ida's imaginary friend, Dotty, goes to school
with her each day. When Ida's classmates tease her about Dotty, Ida
finds an unexpected ally in her teacher.
ISBN 978-0-8109-8962-7
[1. Imaginary playmates—Fiction. 2. Teacher-student relationships—Fiction.
3. Nursery schools—Fiction. 4. Schools—Fiction.] I. Denos, Julia, ill. II. Title.
PZ7.P3163Do 2010
[E]—dc22
2009047418

Text copyright © 2010 Erica S. Perl
Illustrations copyright © 2010 Julia Denos

Book design by Chad W. Beckerman

Printed and bound in China
10 9 8 7 6 5 4 3 2 1

Abrams Books for Young Readers are available at
special discounts when purchased in quantity for
premiums and promotions as well as fundraising or
educational use. Special editions can also be
created to specification. For details, con-
tact specialmarkets@abramsbooks.com or the
address below.

ABRAMS
THE ART OF BOOKS SINCE 1949
115 West 18th Street
New York, NY 10011
www.abramsbooks.com

When Ida started school,
she took her new lunch box . . .

. . . and Dotty.

During Choice Time, Ida found out there were even more noses in her class. Pete and Repeat came to school with Max. They were twins, but not the identical kind.

Spike was Benny's. She had razor-sharp teeth, but Benny swore she would never really hurt anyone.

Keekoo was tiny. She swung back and forth on Katya's braids, chattering all day long.

And there was Dotty, who kept mostly to herself, nibbling the rug.

Dotty occasionally poked people with her horns when she got restless. Pete and Repeat occasionally refused to share. Spike occasionally growled when she missed her nap. And Keekoo occasionally had to be told to let someone else have a turn talking.

But, all in all, everyone in Ms. Raymond's
room got along pretty well that fall.

When Ida went back to school after the winter
holidays, she took her not-so-new lunch box . . .

. . . and Dotty.

"Ida! Hey, Ida!" yelled Katya. "Like my birthday haircut?"

Ida nodded. "Where's Keekoo?" she asked.

"Ida!" scolded Katya. "That's for babies." She looked around, then whispered, "I still keep her in my pocket sometimes."

With a laugh, Katya ran off. Ida chased after her.

Dotty tried to catch up, but the snow made it hard.

In a few months, the green finally returned.

Now when Ida went to school, she took her NEW new lunch box . . .

. . . and Dotty.

Max said Pete and Repeat had moved away.
When Ida asked Benny if Spike still took
naps, Benny said, "Who?"
And Keekoo was long gone.

Then one day, on the swings, Katya said,
"What's that blue string?"

"Nothing," said Ida, wadding it up in a ball.

"Didn't that used to be a leash for . . . what
was her name? Spotty?"

"Dotty," Ida corrected.

"You don't still HAVE her, do you?"

"No," said Ida, too quickly.

Katya stared at Ida. Then she ran off laughing.

Ida stopped swinging.
Dotty shuffled over, chewing on a dandelion.
"Go away!" hissed Ida.
Dotty's ear twitched at a fly. She blinked,
but she didn't budge.

Ida threw the string on the ground. Dotty brought it back to her.

Ida tried to ignore her. But Dotty wouldn't leave her side.

Just then, Katya strolled by, arm in arm with another girl from their class.

"Hey, I-DA!" Katya called out, elbowing her new friend. "I-DA! I think your shoe's untied." The girls giggled.

Ida felt her face get hot.

All of a sudden, Dotty gave a huge tug, yanking
the string out of Ida's hand. She lowered her head
and charged.

WHAM!!!

She crashed into Katya, sending her
sprawling onto the ground.

After school, Ms. Raymond asked Ida to stay for a minute.

"Tell me about Dotty," said Ms. Raymond.

Ida considered telling Ms. Raymond that Dotty was a girl from another class. Or that Dotty was a big dog who had come snarling into the schoolyard. Or that Dotty was an angry rhino who had escaped from the zoo.

But when she opened her mouth, no words came out.

Ms. Raymond tried again. "Do you think you could explain to Dotty that we don't behave like that at school?"

Ida nodded.

"Good," said Ms. Raymond. Then she took something from her desk.

"I'm guessing you want this back," she said.

Ida stared at the red string, then at her teacher.

Ms. Raymond looked puzzled. Then she laughed and said, "Oh, I'm sorry. That one's mine." She put the red string down and handed Dotty's blue string to Ida.

At the door, Ida paused. "Ms. Raymond?" she wanted to ask.
But when she saw the red string dangling off her teacher's
desk, she didn't need to anymore. Instead she waved good-bye
and went outside . . .

...to find Dotty.